This book is based on an
original idea by David Lodge
and is dedicated to Hardy.

First published in Great Britain in 2001 by Bloomsbury Publishing Plc
38 Soho Square, London, W1V 5DF

Copyright (c) Katherine Lodge 2001
The moral right of the author/illustrator has been asserted

A CIP catalogue record of this book is available from the British Library
ISBN 0 7475 5082 4

Printed and bound in Hong Kong by South China Printing Co.

1 3 5 7 9 10 8 6 4 2

Katherine Lodge

Eugene
THE PLANE-SPOTTER

BLOOMSBURY
CHILDREN'S
BOOKS

Eugene loved planes.
He played with toy planes.
He even played at **being** a plane.

Whenever he could,
Eugene went to the airport
to do a spot of plane-spotting.

One Sunday on his way to the airport, Eugene stopped at Caesar's Pizza Palace. As he opened the door Mr Caesar cried out,

Eugene rushed home to pack.
And this is what he put in his suitcase:
5 pairs of underpants
1 toothbrush
4 plane-spotter T-shirts
1 plane-spotters' manual
1 rubber duck
1 inflatable plane
lots of socks
1 camera (loaded)

and a passport!

One week later Eugene boarded
a BIG wide-bodied plane.
It was the greatest day of his life.

He ate an aeroplane meal.

He drank four tomato juices,

and he ate three packets of peanuts.

He looked out of the window.
Everything seemed so small.

After the plane had landed, the first thing
Eugene spotted was his luggage.

Everywhere he went,
Eugene spotted planes.

He spotted them over
the Eiffel Tower,

and high above the Alps . . .

...roaring over
the Leaning Tower of Pisa...

...and in between the pyramids of Egypt.

Eugene spotted planes over the onion domes of Moscow . . .

... above the top of Mount Fuji ...

. . . and across the blue skies of Hawaii.

He spotted planes over the skyscrapers of New York . . .

Marry me ~ Helen ~

. . . and he was still spotting
them when he landed back home.
All too soon, Eugene's
fantastic journey was over.

Next day, Eugene
phoned his friends.
"I've been all
around the world!
Come and see
my holiday snaps."

Planes, planes and even **more** planes.

Well, Eugene **is** a plane-spotter.

PARIS

GENEVA

PISA

NEW YORK

HAWAII